Clarkston School Library

WITHDRAWN

T5-AQQ-293

WITHDRAWN

The Berenstain Bears
and the
MISSING HONEY

There's no case too hard,
no case too tough,
for the Bear Detectives
and their hound dog, Snuff!

BEAR
DETECTIVES

3/20/01

A FIRST TIME READER™

The Berenstain Bears and the MISSING HONEY

Stan & Jan Berenstain

Random House 🏠 New York

Copyright © 1987 by Berenstains, Inc. All rights reserved under International and Pan-American Copyright Conventions. Published in the United States by Random House, Inc., New York, and simultaneously in Canada by Random House of Canada Limited, Toronto.

Library of Congress Cataloging-in-Publication Data: Berenstain, Stan. The Berenstain bears and the missing honey. (A first time reader) SUMMARY: Sister Bear, Brother Bear, Cousin Fred, and his hound Snuff search for the thief who stole Papa Bear's blackberry honey. [1. Mystery and detective stories. 2. Bears—Fiction. 3. Stories in rhyme] I. Berenstain, Jan. II. Title. III. Series: Berenstain, Stan. First time reader. PZ8.3.B4493Bgh 1987 [E] 87-4549 ISBN: 0-394-89133-3 (trade); 0-394-99133-8 (lib. bdg.)

Manufactured in the United States of America

28 29 30

Papa's blackberry honey
is not in the jar!
Whoever took it
cannot have gone far.
"We'll find it, Papa,"
Sister Bear said.
Then Brother Bear whistled
for Cousin Fred.

Blackberry
Honey

Cousin Fred came
with his sniffer hound, Snuff.
He also had
their detective stuff.

The Bear Detectives
looked all around.

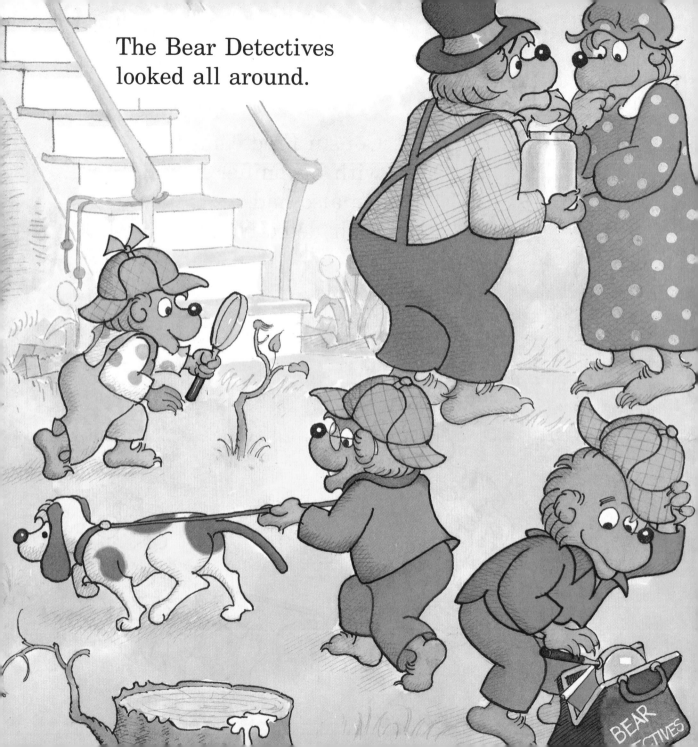

Here are some of the clues
they found:

some fur,

some wax...

and a bit of cloth
that was red and yellow.

"Great!" said Papa.
"These clues will help us
find the fellow!"

"Ask Owl," said Mama.
"It's my belief
he might very well
have seen the thief."
"Tut, tut!" said Papa.
"What can he say?
Why, that sleepy old owl
sleeps all day!"

That's when Snuff started sniffing the air. "He's onto the scent!" shouted Papa Q. Bear.

Snuff smelled blackberries
when he sniffed at the scent.
"Ruff!" said Snuff,
and away they all went.

"Be careful, now,"
said Papa Bear.
"That honey thief
could be anywhere!
Ah! The scent
is coming from
right over there!"

"Oh, no!" said Sister. "Wait, Papa! Stop! That is Beartown's fanciest shop!"

But Papa and Snuff
burst into a room
where the fancy shop sold
BLACKBERRY PERFUME—

and many other kinds as well....
What a mess! What a smell!

"Excuse me, madam.
Sorry about that—
Come, cubs!" said Papa
as he tipped his hat.

"Our search for the thief
has just begun.
The honey thief
could be anyone.

"Bear Detectives,
you may relax.
The key to the crime
is our bit of wax!"

Then Papa and Snuff
dashed into that store—
right past a GONE FISHING
sign on the door.

The detectives were stumped.
But then on the breeze
came a scent so strong,
it made Snuff sneeze.

AH CHOO!

"Look at that shirt!
It's red and yellow!
Just like the clue
from the robber fellow!"

"But, Papa," said Brother,
"that's not the shirt of a HE.
The clothes on that line
are the clothes of a SHE!"

"Son, it wouldn't matter
if it were my own mother.
A thief's a thief!"
said Papa to Brother.

Then the crook of a cane
came out from a wall.
It tripped Papa up.
It made Papa fall.

"I've something to tell you, Papa," said Brother. "This is Grizzly Gran's place! She IS your own mother!"

Again no honey,
in spite of a clue!
Snuff had sniffed
Gran's blackberry stew!
So they headed home,
tired and sad—
the three Bear Detectives,
Snuff, and Dad.

But wait! Has Snuff once more
picked up a scent?
Up the front steps
of the tree house he went!

Up to the bedroom
where Ma and Pa slept.
Into the drawer
where Pa's things were kept.

"What is it?" cried Fred.
"What is it, old fellow?"
Snuff held up something
that was red and yellow!

"Hmm," said Fred.
"How strange. How funny.
This pajama top smells
like blackberry honey!"

"Here," said Brother,
"let me have a look—
the bit of cloth matches!"
Was Papa the crook?

"Clues do not lie,"
Sister Bear said.
"Look! The fur matches too!"
whispered Cousin Fred.

"Me, the thief? That's crazy!"
cried Pa with a howl.
That's when they heard
from sleepy old Owl.

"He carried a candle
down to the shed,
drank up the honey,
and went back to bed!"

THE CLOTH

THE WAX

"I didn't dare wake him.
His sleep was so deep!"

"The case is solved!
No case is too tough
for the Bear Detectives
and our good sniffer, Snuff!"